THIS BOOK BELONGS
TO
C. Abel

children's
choice®

FROM
THE LIBRARY OF

Brittany

READ IT. LOVE IT. RETURN IT

JEAN DE BRUNHOFF

THE STORY

OF

BABAR

the little elephant

Translated from the French by Merle S. Haas
Random House — New York

 A Children's Choice® Book Club Edition from Macmillan Book Clubs, Inc.

The Babar Books

The Story of Babar
The Travels of Babar
Babar the King
Babar and Zéphir
Babar and His Children
Babar and Father Christmas
Babar's Cousin: That Rascal Arthur
Babar's Picnic
Babar's Fair
Babar and the Professor
Babar's Castle
Babar's French Lessons
Babar Comes to America
Babar's Spanish Lessons
Babar Loses His Crown
Babar's Trunk
Babar's Birthday Surprise
Babar's Other Trunk
Babar Visits Another Planet
Meet Babar and His Family
Babar's Bookmobile
Babar and the Wully-Wully
Babar Saves the Day

Copyright 1933, and renewed 1961, by Random House, Inc.

ISBN 0-590-75748-2

Printed in the United States of America.

In the great forest a little elephant is born. His
name is Babar. His mother loves him very much.
She rocks him to sleep with her trunk while sing-
ing softly to him.

Babar has grown bigger. He now plays with the other little elephants. He

is a very good little elephant. See him digging in the sand with his shell.

Babar is riding happily on his mother's back when
a wicked hunter, hidden behind some bushes,
shoots at them.

The hunter has killed Babar's mother! The
monkey hides, the birds fly away, Babar cries.
The hunter runs up to catch poor Babar.

Babar runs away because he
is afraid of the hunter. After
several days, very tired indeed,
he comes to a town . . .

He hardly knows what to
make of it because this is the
first time that he has seen so
many houses.

So many things are new to him! The broad
streets! The automobiles and buses! However, he
is especially interested in two gentlemen he
notices on the street.

He says to himself: "Really, they are very well
dressed. I would like to have some fine clothes,
too! I wonder how I can get them?"

Luckily, a very rich Old Lady who has always been fond of little elephants understands right away that he is longing for a fine suit. As she likes to make people happy, she gives him her purse. Babar says to her politely: "Thank you, Madam."

Without wasting any time, Babar goes into a big store. He enters the elevator. It is such fun to ride up and down in this funny box, that he rides all the way up ten times and all the way down ten times. He did not want to stop but the elevator boy finally said to him: "This is not a toy, Mr. Elephant. You must get out and do your shopping. Look, here is the floorwalker."

Babar then

a shirt
with a collar
and tie,

a suit of a
becoming shade
of green,

buys himself:

then a
handsome
derby hat,

and also
shoes with
spats.

Well satisfied with his purchases
and feeling very elegant indeed,
Babar now goes to the photog-
rapher to have his picture taken.

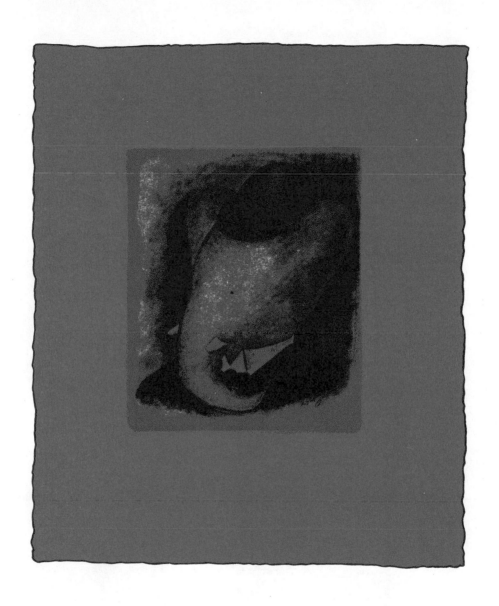

And here is his photograph.

Babar dines with his friend the Old Lady.
She thinks he looks very smart in his new
clothes. After dinner, because he is tired,
he goes to bed and falls asleep very quickly.

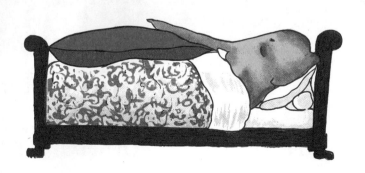

Babar now lives at the Old Lady's house.
In the mornings, he does setting-up exer-
cises with her, and then he takes his bath.

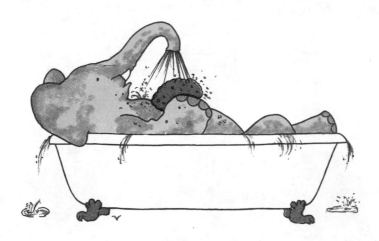

He goes out for an automobile ride every day. The Old Lady
has given him the car. She gives him whatever he wants.

A learned professor gives him lessons. Babar pays
attention and does well in his work. He is a good
pupil and makes rapid progress.

In the evening, after dinner, he tells the Old
Lady's friends all about his life in the great forest.

However, Babar is not quite happy, for he misses playing in the great forest with his little cousins and his friends, the monkeys. He often stands at the window, thinking sadly of his childhood, and cries when he remembers his mother.

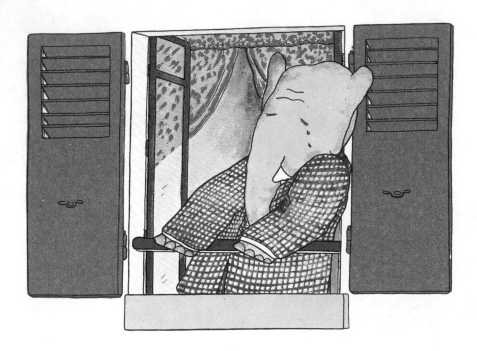

Two years have passed. One day during his walk
he sees two little elephants coming toward him.
They have no clothes on. "Why," he says in
astonishment to the Old Lady, "it's Arthur and
Celeste, my little cousins!"

Babar kisses them affectionately and hurries
off with them to buy them some fine clothes.

He takes them to a pastry shop to eat some
good cakes.

Meanwhile, in the forest, the elephants are calling and hunting high and low for Arthur and Celeste, and their mothers are worried.

Fortunately, in flying over the town, an old marabou bird has seen them and comes back quickly to tell the news.

The mothers of Arthur and Celeste have come to the town to fetch them. They are very happy to have them back, but they scold them just the same because they ran away.

Babar makes up his mind to go back with Arthur
and Celeste and their mothers to see the great
forest again. The Old Lady helps him to pack
his trunk.

They are all ready to start. Babar kisses the Old Lady good-bye. He would be quite happy to go if it were not for leaving her. He promises to come back some day. He will never forget her.

They have gone. . . . There is no room in the car for the mothers, so they run behind, and lift up their trunks to avoid breathing the dust. The Old Lady is left alone. Sadly she wonders: "When shall I see my little Babar again?"

Alas, that very day, the King of the elephants
had eaten a bad mushroom.

It poisoned him and he became ill, so ill that he died. This was a great calamity.

After the funeral the three oldest elephants were holding a meeting to choose a new King.

Just then they hear a noise. They turn around. Guess what they see! Babar arriving in his car and all the elephants running and shouting: "Here they are! Here they are! Hello, Babar! Hello, Arthur! Hello, Celeste! What beautiful clothes! What a beautiful car!"

Then Cornelius, the oldest of all the elephants, spoke in his quavering voice: "My good friends, we are seeking a King. Why not choose Babar? He has just returned from the big city, he has learned so much living among men, let us crown him King." All the other elephants thought that Cornelius had spoken wisely and eagerly they await Babar's reply.

"I want to thank you one and all," said Babar, "but before accepting your proposal, I must explain to you that, while we were traveling in the car, Celeste and I became engaged. If I become your King, she will be your Queen."

"Long live Queen Celeste!

Long live King Babar!"

cry all the elephants without a moment's hesitation. And thus it was that Babar became King.

"You have good ideas," said Babar to Cornelius. "I will therefore make you a general, and when I get my crown, I will give you my hat. In a week I shall marry Celeste. We will then have a splendid party in honor of our marriage and our coronation." Then, turning to the birds, Babar asks them to go and invite all the animals to the festivities, and he tells the dromedary to go to the town and buy some beautiful wedding clothes.

The wedding guests begin to arrive. The dromedary returns with the bridal costumes just in the
nick of time for the ceremony.

After the wedding and the coronation

everybody dances merrily.

The festivities are over, night has fallen, the stars
have risen in the sky. King Babar and Queen Celeste
are indeed very happy.

Now the world is asleep. The guests have gone home, happy, though tired from too much dancing. They will long remember this great celebration.

And now King Babar and Queen Celeste, both eager
for further adventures, set out on their honeymoon
in a gorgeous yellow balloon.